MY PET FEET

Josh Funk

Billy Yong

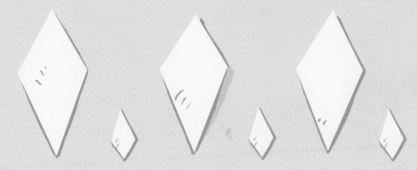

SIMON & SCHUSTE BOOKS FO YOUNG EADES

New Yok London Toonto Sydney New Delhi

Today, I woke up and was about to feed my pet when—

"Doodles?" I asked. "Is that you?" What was happening? I scanned high and low. And then I saw it.

The alphabet on my wall was incomplete!

PQ STUVWXY

"The lette—,
I mean, the *symbol* between
Q and *S* . . .

it's gone!"

I looked at Doodles.

"Ahh. I see. Without the . . .

FE_ _ET

. . . he's become FEET."

I didn't know how to fix this, but I had to do something to save him.

Maybe my buddy Lucas could help.

and almost bumped into a policewoman on the back of a galloping hose.

KEEP OFF THE LAWN

Inside the family bake shop, Lucas's mom took a bead pan out of the oven.

"Lucas," I said.
"What's going on?"

Lucas scowled at me.

Most days he's my pal, but today he was a fiend. I hugged Doodles as I backed outside.

All the townspeople acted as if this was just a typical day.

Out of the blue, a flock of COWS began chasing us.

We fled to the town hall, but couldn't get in the doo.

With the cows still behind me, I climbed a massive cane that loomed above the building.

As I suspected, cows don't like heights.

High above the town, Doodles clung to me with all ten toes.

To save him, I needed to know what happened
to the eighteenth symbol
of the alphabet.

Did it fade out of existence?

P Q **?** S T

Doubtful.

Did it get used up?

Not likely.

Vowels get used most. I could still say

A E I O U.

And sometimes

Y

Maybe someone took it? But who? And why? I was stumped.
"I don't want to have pet feet until the end of time!" I wailed.

Doodles gave me the saddest pout imaginable.

"Doodles, I didn't mean it. I'm so—"

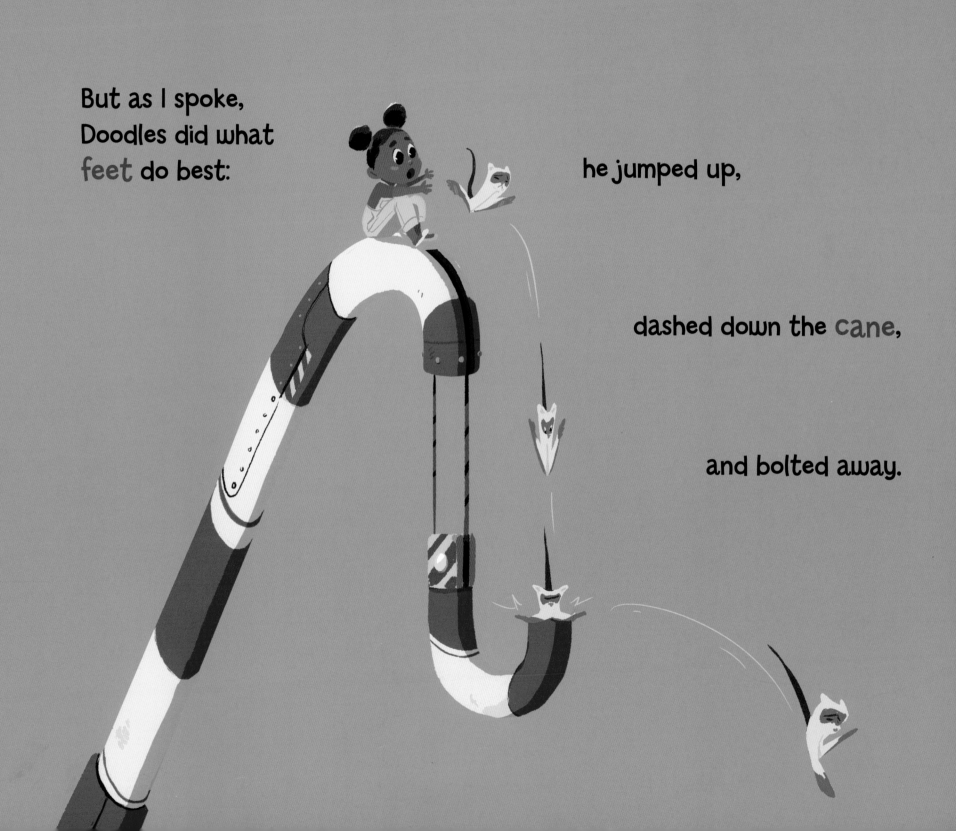

But as I spoke,
Doodles did what
feet do best:

he jumped up,

dashed down the cane,

and bolted away.

"Come back!"
I shouted.

I chased Doodles
past a fog and toad,

by the old babbling
book, down a tail,

and into a gassy field.

Just like the missing piece of the alphabet,
Doodles had vanished.

This whole situation was a massive catast—
A huge disaste—
A bad thing.

But I couldn't give up.

I followed the faint sound of footsteps and finally found Doodles at the seashoe.

I avoided tiny cabs scuttling along the sand,

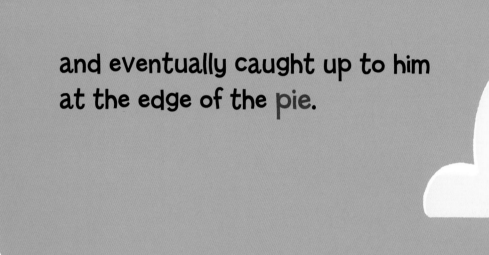

and eventually caught up to him
at the edge of the pie.

Pie 3.14

"Doodles, please accept my apology. You could be an animal, you could be *feet*—but you will *always* be a fantastic companion!"

Doodles hopped up.

"Aww, I love you, too."

All of a sudden, he dove into the ocean.

"R," said one of the scallywags.

"R?" said another.

The pirate captain handed me a treasure chest.
"Take them," he growled.

"We wanted to be the only ones in the world who could
utter the letter R, but now it's all me mateys say!"

The trunk overflowed with a plethora of pilfered *R*s!

I reached in and delivered
two to Doodles.

Immediately,
he transformed.

What a day! The *R* fiasco was resolved and the town was now repaired.

Doodles lay resting directly over my heart. My pet ferret was right where he belonged.

Ready to retire, I could finally relax and catch some . . .

Oh no!

How did I miss it before?
Where are all the—

For my pets, Dobby, Hiro Nakamura, Lincoln Hawk, and Katnip Everdeen,
none of whom, to my knowledge, are or have ever been feet
—J. F.

For my beautiful girls, Rachel and Ellie
—B. Y.

SIMON & SCHUSTER BOOKS FOR YOUNG READERS
An imprint of Simon & Schuster Children's Publishing Division
1230 Avenue of the Americas, New York, New York 10020
Text © 2022 by Josh Funk
Illustration © 2022 by Billy Yong
Edited by Kendra Levin • Book design by Chloë Foglia © 2022 by Simon & Schuster, Inc.
For information about special discounts for bulk purchases, please contact Simon & Schuster Special Sales
at 1-866-506-1949 or business@simonandschuster.com.
The Simon & Schuster Speakers Bureau can bring authors to your live event. For more information or to book an event,
contact the Simon & Schuster Speakers Bureau at 1-866-248-3049 or visit our website at www.simonspeakers.com.
The text for this book was set in Billy. • The illustrations for this book were rendered digitally.
Manufactured in China • 0522 SCP
First Edition
2 4 6 8 10 9 7 5 3 1
Library of Congress Cataloging-in-Publication Data
Names: Funk, Josh, author. | Yong, Billy, illustrator.
Title: My pet feet / Josh Funk ; illustrated by Billy Yong.
Description: First edition. | New York : Simon & Schuster Books for Young Readers, [2022] | Audience: Ages 4-8. | Audience: Grades K-1. |
Summary: After awakening to find that her pet ferret is now pet feet, a budding detective discovers
that the letter "R" has disappeared and its absence is causing chaos throughout her town.
Identifiers: LCCN 2020055522 | ISBN 9781534486003 (hardcover) | ISBN 9781534486010 (ebook)
Subjects: CYAC: Alphabet—Fiction. | City and town life—Fiction. | Lost and found possessions—Fiction. | Mystery and detective stories. | Humorous stories.
Classification: LCC PZ7.1.F95 My 2022 | DDC [E]—dc23 • LC record available at https://lccn.loc.gov/2020055522